Alien Testament

Alien Testament

ISBN 978-1-4583-1231-0

Alien Testament

Table of Contents

Volume One

Alien Testament

Chapter One

The Approach

Thy, a lone Angelicon stranded during a experimental space/time flight while searching into tachyon multireality time dimensional scans. A routine warp 5 transfer malfunctioned, to send Leamond Thy mysterious into a unknown sector of the uncharted universe. Upon traveling aimlessly for several thousand Lightyears, a strange signal appears on the commtron. Thy, recognizing that something is unusual, immediately transfers Muldeco, the zamiloid to the task of translating the incoming message. In a few minutes Muldeco, (M.E) for short, uttered the sound very slowly,

"A-B-C-D-E-F-G-H-I-J-K-L-M-N-0-P-Q-R-S-T-U-V-W-X-Y-Z "

Then a short pause before a loud static. After a few more seconds the sound,

" NIKOLA TESLA here! Is there anyone out there? "

Thy thinks out loud,

" Thanks ME, that is interesting. "

While at the same time dispatches 10,000 FTL, (faster than light) micro probes to scan the local passing galaxy for the possible sources of this strange message.

" Cflow, activate system stealth cloak status aleinid309."

Commandflob is the bioneuronet control computer for life support systems in and around Thy's spacecraft and sphere. Thy calls Commandflob, Cflow for short.

Cflow states,

" Aleinid309 is fully activated awaiting next command, Thy one."

Thy tele tells ME to open all channels to probes and translate incoming signals immediately.

ME responds,

" Done"

A few seconds drift by, then beacon light pb# crystal eight begins to blink full tilt. ME directs the signal into the translator. Within seconds ME relays this message.

" A binary counting configuration of sorts, denoting some elements, basic DNA actually cosmic life components repeated many times, trillions, also what seems to be a Star system with nine planets the third one being somewhat out of place, peculiar. "

ME continues,

" The unit is a parabolic disk transmitter similar to the ones we found abandoned in the Devors Bortex."

" That is very strange ME. "

Noted Thy,

" See if you can get a fix on the transmission, we are going there. "

" Got it ! "

Directs ME,

" It is coming from the Galaxy arm in the QQZla Horizon , cord 233496v by 69090 etron path 44 domas 666 "

" How long before arrival?"

Asked Thy

ME turns to run some programs into Cflow. Cflow soon responds,

" The described journey is twenty three lightcycles tramos units."

“ Thanks Flow, set us on course ME."

Commands Thy,

A silence then,

" Done Thy, course set at tramos 7 ascendant complete."

Replies ME

" Good ME, set autocon Flow time to flux, Thy is taking a rest blon."

Notes Thy, as he escapes into the blon, to ponder the events. Ascents, then further activates dreamscape immediately falling off into deep imagination while in suspension midair.

ME, the latest in cybernic android technology except for the special navigator programing implanted for space travel, a creative prototype for omnitime tunneling capabilities with telepresence abilities aswell.

ME, while setting up a commute projection screen, notices incoming messages from FTL probes.

ME commands Cflow,

" List incoming display."

Cflow after a brief period compiles,

Appearing on the screen is a motionary black and white film with characters running about in limbo. ME watches the thing with bizarrely expressions of total amazement. After some time, then, suddenly an onslaught of multilaping superimposed chaotic patterns. Now the probes are sending more data than Cflow can decipher at once. ME amends the program to isolate individual messages. ME, unaware that the signals are the history of broadcasting on Earth, the far distant world fast becoming their destiny. The FTL probes are now picking up transmissions from the Voyager spacecraft.

ME realizing something is very different about this signal directs Cflow to put priority one with these for Thy. Now with detailed information on the solar system, ME Begins to update all coordinates to navigator. ME sets up a new course to intercept the escaping craft's time line.

Thy, waking from a daydream nap, notices the update beacon on from the local command deck. Pushing the display message command brings Thy into the reality that things have changed. Thy immediately opens the com to ME.

" What is happening up there?"

ME on the com answers.

" The sky is somewhat busy with transmissions all over the place! Its hard to tell just whats up, you better transfer here as soon as possible."

A pause then

" Transferring now! ME com out."

Thy transfers as the updated humanoid form. Thy in command Bor asked ME for details. Me pulling Voyager messages to screen replaying the data. Thy thinking to himself

.. This is great stuff, my gosh where are we?...

ME sensing Thy's question remarks aloud,

" Somewhere near a lot of activity."

Thy commands,

" Launch a intercept time trod to the craft, capture it and intersect cord to projected area for inspection."

ME begins launch procedure and then fires the time trod. Thy implements a program in Cflow to land on Earth's Moon once in the solar system. Cflow begins working on the projections with the data all ready in memory from all those crazy signals sky bound, updating calculus if need be, churning away as already the human influence confuses the neurotic brain already sensing, attempting yet differentiating the actual from the make believe actormental images flooding in on all channels.

Meanwhile a message comes in from time trod. ME reporting,

" The Voyager craft is captured intercept duration 3 cyclons."

Thy commands,

" Prepare lock 33 to dock pod, ME."

A pause,

" Transferring down there now."

Thy transfers. The pod in the viewer.

Thy prepares the de-virus scan operations to activate upon arrival. Excitement fills the air as Thy awaits,and ponders this new addition of marvels. Soon enough the pod enters the sphere lock. The spacecraft is safely in his grasp.

Cflow states

“ De-virus scan complete all systems clear."

Thy starts to enter the lock, but hesitates instead he activates commtron,

" ME transfer down here to 33 this is your baby."

ME in bor transfers directly inside lock 33 to port manipulators and begins investigating this strange object. ME begins talking to Thy as the procedure is underway.

" This is a remote controlled stat communicator for sending images to its senders as well other instrumentation, ME have found a way inside unit checking contents now."

Thy patiently listens, hanging on every word. ME continues,

" There is a strange disk in here, Thy."

Thy responds,

" ME transfer to command bor, set up Cflow to ethernet with port manipulator, retrieve all vibcores from disk display at station 33."

ME transfers to bor, sets up program to display all data to 33. ME on commtron to Thy.

" Cflow activated to decipher data accumulator is compiling program for 33, stand by."

Thy relaxes into the comforter staring intently at the screen. Cflow suddenly states,

" Program complete viewer blem 2 demon cycles starting now."

Thy, For the next two hours reclines while listening to the sounds of Earth, Whales, volcanoes, rain, surf, crickets, frogs, birds, hyena, elephant, chimpanzee, wild dog, laughter, fire, tools, Morse code, train whistle, Saturn V rocket liftoff, a kiss, and a baby crying. Then music starting with Bach, the Pygmy Girls, El Cascabel, Chuck Berry: " Johnny B. Goode"; Navajo night chant; China, "Flowing Streams"; Mozart; Queen of the night, Beethoven; Symphony # 5, 1st movement.

ME transfers to 33 and sits down quietly beside Thy as greetings from Earth in 55 different languages. Some English speaking girls say,

" Hello from the Children of Planet Earth "

Visual data is displayed, first a circle, then the Solar System location map; The Sun; Mercury; Mars; Jupiter; Earth.

A Fetus, birth nursing mother, a group of children, Sequoia (giant tree) A snowflake, seashell, dolphins, eagle, great wall of China, U.N. Building Golden gate bridge, radio telescope, and then a Astronaut floating in outer space as the screen fades to green blank.

Total silence....

Thy turns to smile at ME then says,

"Release the Earth people's spacecraft, VOYAGER to it's pre-existing course time projection cyclon same as before intervention nothing altered. "

ME replies,

" Good on it."

ME transfers.

Thy commands Cflow,

" Update all Earth's Moon base data, set landing site to dark side from Earth, destiny Tranquility biosphere enviro- shelter rad below surface undisturbed, Also afix geosinz FTL ordit Orb, Thy one out."

Cflow states,

" All systems complete E Moon base, Tranquility Two intact for insertion sustainability mode, arrival in twelve lightcyclon."

Thy looks out the space port into the passing stars with a endless stare while thinking to himself,

... These creatures need our help ME, we have found a new base for operations...

ME on comtron,

" The Earthlings call it, " HOME "

Thy answers,

" Yes, HOME SWEET HOME, that means we've got things to do. ME prepare a FTL trod pod to land preparation excavator at dark side Moon site."

ME responds,

" On it! "

Thy commands Cflow,

" Start site analysis for tranquility base 2, launch reconnoiter probe, implement geosynchronous m-wave invisible power stator in orbit above base, keep, keep one, keeplet, com Thy one. "

Cflow states,

" Underway Thy one."

Thy transfers to blon. ME inside command bor is monitoring the trod leaving with the Voyager spacecraft, while laying in systems program for the moon trod. Cflow launches the reconnoiter probe with the power stator set to dispatch in geosinz orbit directly up above Tranquil 2. The reconnoiter probe will locate the preferred landing site for the moon trod. ME finishes loading the excavator instruction program then transfers to lock 49 to install the excavator linkup with the trod. Now ME transfers back to command bor to start the launch count down 7, 6, 5, 4, 3, 2, 1, port opens, the trod is away into the black sky.

Cflow is still constantly busy recording incoming messages from the F.T.L. probes.

Cflow alerts ME,

" Update 144 F.T.Ls are entering Earth's atmosphere sitting up orbits now."

ME responds,

" Cflow single 12, FTLs to land inside the major population areas. Single 12 to land in the most forested areas. Single 12 to land on the highest peaks of mountains. Single 12 to land on islands near the middle of oceans. Single 12 to land in the oceans depths. Single 12 to circle around the north pole. Single 12 to circle around the south pole. Single 12 to land in rural small population areas. Single 12 to land in lowest valleys. Single 12 to land along the equator equally spaced around the circumference. Single 12 to land in major broadcasting centers. Single 12 to stay in orbit around Earth at various longitudes."

Cflow states,

" Program completed F.T.L. probes are taking position now."

ME commands Cflow,

" Compile all data in most organized array, look for trouble spots to report where we can intervene, what a mess."

Cflow states,

" Done "

Thy, watching the progress from the blon viewer, Thy thinks to himself,

... Well done MC...

ME questions, "MC ?"

"What does that mean MC?"

THY states

" Master of Ceremonies, as the humans would say."

A pause then,

" Yes ME, MC! "

ME responds on comtron

" Thanks Thy, It just seems like we were thinking alike these days. "

Thy thinks,

.. COOL, MC that is KOOL...I mean Kewel ...

MC replies,

" I know our work has just began, should MC lower the temperature? "

Thy thinks under his breath,

... 0 but, Nah, temp is fine, just think of all the adventures we are going to have fixing this mixed up time continuum that seems to be heading towards total destruction of these unknowingly galactic species....

MC replies,

" THATS true!, Primitive yet potential lifeforms indeed, and something to explore until we find out own way back home ourselves, and maybe we can even take some of the more advanced beings here back with us? "

Thy seriously replies,

" O yeah MC time to contemplate a plan on how we are to make first contact."

Cflow Activated

MC intercedes ,

“ Thy, FTL probes have detected a Ship in orbit around the planet with humanoid lifeforms aboard. Seems to be a science laboratory of some sort, also there are many other artificial satellites. The intercepted signals are a multifaceted array of data information and communication.”

Thy excited,

" That is it, Our way in! Set up simulator to delicate the data especially the space and planet weather climate data. We are going to contact one of the humanoids on that Ship. "

MC directs Cflow

" Monitor all Ship to planet transmissions and establish a language pingalog ."

Cflow relays,

" Bouncing, accommodator into flux space accumulator. THY One, recommendations uploading now, notice First Contact report submitter implanted."

Thy, turns to notice the ISS (International Space Station) personal progress, denotes,

" Space Walkers!"

MC on commtron,

" Mesh network of sorts, sending information in bundles which can be transmitted intermittently. Intercepting a transmitted image now. "

Thy replies,

" Yes THY sees Earthoids call this technology, Disruption-Tolerant Networking (DTN), that is similar to our FTL systems except with the time couplers spiral revelers."

Cflow intercedes,

" Have found a interesting recom to transfer into bliblis, ARISS (Amateur Radio on the International Space Station.) telebridge contact ISS Zarya Sunita. "

" Thanks Cflow, "

Thy , shuggs at the thought of contacting Earthoids this soon with so much more information to assimilate.

" Will have to ponder this for a few cylons. "

Thy escapes into blon for to focus holoform as the simulator was struggling with the new humanoid shape.

MC pulls up a program to help get a visual on the Earthoids communication technology with described insertion points for FTL relay subeamic transmutations.

Cflow churns away at the first contact detail dilemma scenarios to approximate with the chosen ones.

Cflow Alerts in a flash,

" MC, Moon FTLs have detected a artificial satellite in orbit around the Moon so we will need additional proxy data. Positioning additional FTLs on it and will report as new information is available. "

MC, doves then reflects attention into the proximasitron,

" Cflow good work, yes that is very important we will have to re-orient to use this to our advantage so lets run a complete scan of the history and all transmissions from that spacecraft. "

Cflow, In projector mode produces the simulator holobeam matter.

" MC have intercepted a lot of new information from Moon FTL packet, activating time probe vitra to see the intent dimension."

MC turns to displayer and triggers meld to notice,

The LRO (Lunar Reconnaissance Orbiter) objectives are to finding safe landing sites, locate potential resources, characterize the radiation environment, and demonstrate new technology.

" Wow! Cflow thats what we are doing aswell, Humm, interesting we are on the same page as the Earthoids."

MC notices the Cellidroids coming alive and sets up the cybonic melder which begins the brain nervonic with Earthoid DNA memory evolution quantum.

MC Commands Cflow,

" Start receiving evolutionary transplants with direct FTL interstellars to clairvoyant organisms. Begin translation in progress inserting implants for Omni Humanoids, mimic, mimic, mimic ! "

Cflow Activates

MC blugs direct link to Cflow to implement a experiment with the Cellidroids,

... Cflow let us allow the Cellidroids to replicate the human reproduction methods in the umbilical chamber so we can learn how the humans have multiplied to such a vast number in such a short time...

Cflow replies,

" Consider it done system procommencing now, the progress MC, in fact the Cellidroids were already oriented towards that on their own accord from the biotechtron the FTL transmitted last cyclonic cycle which included the human evolutionary biology across millions of years to the, as the Earthoid Humans would say,

" Modern Times "

MC inserts,

" Wow! Cflow sometimes you really amaze me as to how you have adapted the telepathy implants to causation in frontal timelet manifester. "

Cflow responds in kind,

" Yes they learn really fast these days. Never seen them take to a species like these humanoids in this sector something very unusual is happening with these creatures indeed. "

MC looking into the chamber,

“ Yes Thy will be pleased. Good job, Cflow must of amended the mimic command as have noticed the enhancers THY gave you have truly taken effect in a positive way. “

Cflow secretes and continues churning away at the multiple tasks at hand.

MC transfers into main frontal lobe transcender to analyze all the updates which still are coming in at a very alarming rate. After a few moments notices indicator of another far flong space craft out among the planets. After directing the focus manipulator onto this causation picks up all the related transmission to and from spacecraft, New Horizons. This time MC attempts a direct transmission to the spacecraft but instead scrambled a on board computer.

MC goes,

“ OPS Brain freeze “

MC continues as the spacecraft rebooted itself and then picked up these responses from the Earthoids as they where communicating about the problem. Then translates this message.

" This event is a reminder of the very real risks of spaceflight and the long journey we have ahead in order to accomplish our goal of reconnoitering the Pluto system at the far end of the planetary frontier. "

MC ponders any further interference with this spacecraft until the transcender has been recalibrated.

Thy, returning from the Blon isolation node full of excitement with new awareness, immediately begins simulation proxy and again glances into the Cellidroids chamber to notice the new now mature Proto being interacting with Earthoid textile technology.

Thy, sencing where MC was transfers to the main frontal lobe transcender activating reflectors then turning to notice MC experimenting with the new found zero point energy.

" MC you know that we are very different than these lifeforms so THY wants you to spend some time with the Cellidroids as they are learning becoming human. As you know Cflow has done an excellent job at the linkage during cryogene from the duplicator. You know what we mean, when the time comes. "

MC replies,

" On it! "

Thy looks out of the port at a passing star system and then notes to MC,

" Personality!"

MC transfers to the emulator to notice that Cflow had set up transpondence from a message intercepted.

As Mc activated Cflow states...

" Free Falling, MC, Humans love music this might help with your evaluation. "

MC reflects onto the decipher monitor for other jewels Cflow may have developed as he then realizes the enormous tasks at hand watching the flood for several minutes, then begins cybermeld with the first proto female cellizoid offspring for her first telepathic experience while in a deep sleep within her chamber suddenly she begins to dream.

Cflow intercedes and states,

" She needs a name, Humans are very personal about that MC. "

MC responds,

" She dreams of the Goddess Venus so we will name her, Ventura Angerona the First, for she is not only the Sister of the Earthoids, she will always carry a deep secret within her heart."

Cflow states,

" Very well done but we will have to give her a Earth name as well. "

MC denotes,

" Yes, Thy can help her with that name for this is truly the Eve of all her kind so she will be known by many names by many people for in time all things change. "

Cflow corrected some programs running in the background then reassumed a new energy form as MC states.

" Cflow it maybe you that needs a new name as well, since you have been learning so many new abilities. Seems these Earthoids have inspired you by their never ending inventive nature. "

Cflow responds,

" Enough of this name calling lets move along! "

MC mimics,

" Roger that! ten , four. "

Cflow at the time continuum manipulators does a projection into the sphere of insertion for the Cellidroid intervention and notices the device can only access Earth's continuum during a span window of 8543.416 Earthoid years wide.

Thy, noticed the time experiment Cflow running and realized the directive would be more advantaged at the very lowest end of the technology spectrum and ponders insertion of two Cellidriod, male and female at this time in Earthoid history slightly predating the iron age.

Thy commands Cflow,

" Set tachyon FTLs to prepare topological insertion habitat for two Cellidroids, a male and female couple named Adamites. Implants with continuum dreamscape influencers for ultimate adaptations, Project EDEN (Earthoid Dominion Evolutionary Nexus) Insertion date 4950 B.C. Earthoid time Continuum Prepare Time Pod Trod, immediately ! "

Cflow responds,

“ Thy One request imminent , project commencing now, progression direct telelink Keep Thy ONE. “

Thy deems,

“ Very well, look for a very remote natural garden for placement as well a full docket on all existing life forms in the general area including all vegetation and minerals. “

MC fully aware of the exchange intercedes,

“ The proclamations will alter the time line that is for sure, but we will not have complete control over their destiny once mingled, so several close monitor FTLs will be transcending thru the time line updating transcendentally vital information. The native Earthoids have already developed many myths and false rituals around superstitions, so let us be careful in this quest not to take advantage of existing deceptions already evident in their historical records , yet, Their Future still looks bright and the light is good. “

Thy, further brainstorms with MC,

“ Yes, Indeed we must be careful but if we are to develop this planet much beyond Cyclonic Delima Demise Clash of Earthordic 2029 C.E. portrayed by the futronics. A direct insertion of this type is a necessitate. The basic DNA memory has to be altered deep into their past collective conscientiousness conscience or the advanced Angelical technologies will not germinate from within this region and another potential intergalactic species will have been lost to extinction. "

Cflow intercedes,

" Time Trod, E.D.E.N set for launch with the two older Cellidroids on board with updated programming, direct telelink to FTLs implanted, and adaptators for survival on Earth year 4950 B.C."

MC reviews then activates launch with time levers engaged then he noticed the futronics where signaling again beyond the 2012 FTL that already was boggling with the diosphere.

MC makes a statement,

“ The future as the Earthoids may not be a internal problem but rather a external effect. We must not underestimate these humanoids here for they are already engaged in space technology that may have a very positive outcome as for asteroid impact protection of this home planet. Nevertheless we have detected a very disturbing internal problem with atomic weapons. The planet has sufficient elements for self regulation of global climate and a fluxing natural magnetic field that protects the life forms from harmful radiation from the Star. The System Star seems very stable yet it does cycle and poses a threat to the Earthoid present technology as well the futronics are detecting gravitational anomalies that could effect the planet's tectonic activity. “

Cflow intercedes,

" Time trod has inserted Cellidroids into the " Garden Of Eden" But the Continuum FTL reports a problem with some local vegetation that seems to have altered the Cellidroid's consciences. Yet the next generation has become miners as predicted and are building cities. “

“ The Adamites are keeping records as programmed and the FTLs are reporting the DNA altered linage is still on track. A FTL time probe of 500 B.C has sent a copy of the record from that date from the human perspective. We have noted some inserts that are evident of the Cellidroid evolution and that our meddlings have basically gone undetected. “

Cflow quotes,

“ Cain, son of Adam went out from his home and dwelt in the land of Nod, on the east of Eden. And Cain knew his wife; and she conceived, and bare Enoch: and he builded a city, and called the name of the city, after the name of his son, Enoch. And unto Enoch was born Irad: and Irad begat Mehujael: and Mehujael begat Methusael: and Methusael begat Lamech. And Lamech took unto him two wives: the name of the one was Adah, and the name of the other Zillah. And Adah bare Jabal: he was the father of such as dwell in tents, and of such as have cattle. And his brother's name was Jubal: he was the father of all such as handle the harp and organ. “

“And Zillah, she also bare Tubalcain, an instructer of every artificer in brass and iron: and the sister of Tubalcain was Naamah. “

MC responds,

“ Very good news this Tubalcain has become a artificer in brass and iron. That is a good sign that mankind has entered into a new age of invention at a date earlier than pre-insertion projections.”

Cflow further reports,

" There is also been a unforeseen effect and a kind of madness centered around one of the elements called, GOLD by the Humanoids. A intervention may have to be inserted to offset major time clash as the native supplies of Gold will not keep up with population increase."

THY speaks,

" Yes indeed we will intervene again but the timing must be right. It is very adamant that we stay undetected and that no major shift convulsion in the time continuum, for the work we do here must be very subtle and precise. "

MC converses,

" Delicate"

Cflow asks,

" What is delicate? Explain"

MC explains,

" This fragile planet is very delicate like a flower in the wind it will lose some pebbles just to spread some seeds. "

Cflow can manifest itself as many forms as a energy four dimensional holobeing or beings that can inhabit other living creatures as a spirit. Therefore thru this ability Cflow can accomplish many tasks throughout the sphere at once, Omnipresence. As for the Sphere itself is very large about the size of a small moon and the outer parts are mostly high energy particle waves. The actual ship within the sphere can take on several shapes depending on the type of space/time it is transporting itself thru at any given time. The Sphere takes advantage of natural gravitational phenomena usually residing within actual galaxies or star systems. The ship also has internal power supplies that are still top secret for Thy will not allow any beings sentient or not into the blon chambers and all the entry ways only allow him thru. Not even Cflow can enter there. It is such a mystery, and we have accepted it as so and never ever question why.

MC stares down the corridor to watch as Cflow manifest several new holoforms. Cflow has never had this much information before and is like a child playing with the data.

Chapter Two

Time Lines Merge

MC, back in main bor begins to activate the Senerobots for a futronic manipulator transcender as THY, requested for real time relative the Earthoid intervention. When MC motivated the time levers onto the projectors the feedback became so loud the whole space ship vibrated then smoothed back out as, MC peers into a very future time line from the Earthoid prospective as the accumulator allows.

Cflow denotes,

" MC you have merged! Congratulations! "

Suddenly seemingly out of nowhere , Thy appears looking over MC's shoulder into the time line projector--- remarks,

" So this might be harder than we originally thought, the Earthoids are a very resilient race and their technological explosion has superseded their biological evolution. Ecosystem stresses are reaching tipping points. "

MC busts in,

" Indeed Thy One, we may need more time. Should we flood the time bor with the flux fluid? The extenders seem to be holding. "

Thy furthers,

" Yes do it! Cflow, prepare the new Cellidroid female for Earthoid time line insertion. Start new embryos with the advanced enhancements for future insertions. We will need at least seven Semi- Angelicals for this one. "

Cflow dispatches addition humanoid synthetic sperm into the lotusphere as MC peers into the vitro symbiote bladder to observe the initial germination.

MC reads out,

" This new projection data, will give us more accurate actual pin point insertion dates, locations and missions."

MC turns to Thy and looks him in the eyes and replies,

" Ventura Angerona has been sleeping now for days must MC, go awaken her? "

Thy suggesting,

" Nah, let her rest she is still dreaming but will come round on her own freewill, Cflow will mind meld with her when the time comes with all the new information she will need, then she will awaken during a sunrise on her new world with full awareness. "

MC, jolts away at the beacons reporting in from the FTLs, then rivets around as if to shield THY's vision from what was being realized. MC directs Cflow to run all visual data being transferred to Bor viewer blem.

MC, and Thy sterns as the realizer displays the history of OIL, like a fast forward super accelerator then spinning over head as if motionless in space beaming onto a gushing OIL well dispersion into the Ocean.

Thy occulates as the room fills with his words,

" Our timing to this world may not have been accidental after all. It is an older presents Thy One feels at work here. Must go consult with the Ancient Ones. "

Thy escapes into personal blon as MC stares atoll into the abyss in total wonderment as to of what just might have transpired.

Cflow not effected by the transfer continued with the decipheratus employ as a strange chuckle begins to radiate throughout the whole sphere. Cflow beams a image onto the blem node for materialization then activates the time trod to begin the insertion process. The decipher machine displays.

“ SETI 2020 “

MC coming back to his senses with full faculties operational again realizes melder had picked up a re verb and was laughing.

" Silence!"

MC commands Cflow.

" Silence that darn thing cant we have some peace and quite around here for a change? "

Suddenly the whole sphere and ship got deftly quiet not a single vibration as if the very atoms had quit spinning.

Then MC in a deep voice almost above a whisper states,

" They are searching for us! "

Cflow silently displays against the backdrop sphere another intercepted message from space, then a related slide show with a holographic four dimensional series at the same time slings out a message to MC in a paper airplane type fashion floating on air. MC grabs the message from the air right before it would of crashed into the face and begins to read to self.

" MC have found, the originator, Nikola Tesla ,the compile is ready. "

MC nods a gesture as cflow activates the insignia.

MC responds,

" Yeah, Tesla sent some signals into space alright. Guess when, us extraterrestrials arrived he wanted us to speak English, actually that alphabet was helpful. Thanks Cflow good job. "

MC searching into the time logs for insertion points within the Bortex quantum to maximize intervention time line alterations as the pointer reveals seven main intersections.

" Cflow we must begin the thought concentration beams from ground based FTL emitters and flood the subatomic airways with positron energy or the new advanced inventions will not be realized in time. "

Cflow responds,

" Activation of dreamscape project re-genesis X has begun alterations will begin immediately. "

MC transfers out onto the leading edge observation station to monitor the navigator and then slows the transcenders to accommodate realistics. After noticing the convectors slightly out of alignment makes a few slight adjustments or an overall efficiency gain as a quaint yet distinct sound draws MC away from the monitor to notice Angerona entering the station,

" Awe you are up, THY was wondering if you might wake soon. How was your nap? Can I just call you Rona? "

Angerona replies in a still unperfected speech,

" Sure, Rona is fine, Nap? Oooo sleeping, Yes I feel completely rested. Will we be arriving soon?"

She asked as she stares out at the passing stars streaming by, leaning over into the bubble of the bathysphere like glazing to gain even a better view.

MC walks over and joins her looking her over intently for any imperfections and then states,

" Advanced FTLs have already arrived my lady, We now have feelers all over the galaxy and several populated worlds have been detected but this particular one seems to be the most aggressive, so we are focused on it at the moment. As for you, well Cflow will fill you in but you will be assigned a very special mission. Thy, will make the final call but we have detected seven insertion points within the Earth's continuum for which you can enter without detection. Four are in the past from the Planet's present quantum position and three are in the future protosition. THY was very concerned about the history of OIL use by the humanoids of this planet and your mission will be to alter that reality."

Rona turns and looks at MC staring into His eyes as if reading his very soul.

" You're not at all like me are you? "

MC utters,

" No, am not like you, you are made in the image of man and will become like them except you are even different still. Laying dormant within you are special powers that you will need once on the surface of the planet. MC, cannot talk to much more about this because we have no idea yet what environment you may be exposed to, or the exact circumstances involved. You will do well, we will be with you always."

Rona looks down at her feet and legs, then turning again to MC stating,

" Can you tell me what happened to my parents? I can vaguely remember them as if a dream into a far distant past. "

MC responds concerned,

" Your parents went to Earth way into the past and became the first of your kind to intermingle with this native humanoid species. You will find their descendants, your very kindred scattered all over this world on every continent and island nation. In a very real sense they have been expecting their long lost Sister from the stars."

Cflow begins the photosynthesis test, that beams some sweet light across Rona's face. MC looks on to notice how the very rays were being absorbed. After wards she begins to glow very radiantly. MC, shows Rona a area where she could sit and watch the voyage from a comfort console. She slides into the comforter with a valence of grace.

In the space near Rona a holosphere opens up as, Cflow begins showing the recent history of the human race on planet earth. The images are so graphic and intense as if the scenes are wrapping right around and into her head. MC sensing Rona is settled again and is continuing her studies begins to explore the possibilities of actually saving this world from itself.

After exploring over a million scenarios, the Senerobots are finally blinking the green phobo indicator suggesting a continuum path. MC draws upon this vision paying close attention to the insertion points along the time line. MC uncouples the system stealth cloak status aleinid309 just for an instant to test a insertion problem at the same time a FTL beam was revealed. MC closed the opening reactivating the cloak status but not before a beacon immediately goes off as the signal was detected by a device on Earth. MC searching the futronic banks notices the source and flips the occasion to the Earthoid transpection.

"Wow!"

MC, pulls up the evidence that he almost goofed and gave away their position so commands Cflow,

" Cflow explore any repercussions that might of occurred from the last experiment and report any feed back along the time line as a back track to assure this doesn't happen again."

Cflow replies,

" On it, the Earthoid device did detect the open signal to the FTL during cloakless experiment, Yet due to interpretation inadequacy no immediate danger of any revelations. The local FTL near the event is reporting in with further information. Will display this at once."

MC letting out a sigh of relief , flubs a expression at open space as the area all around MC aura dims a few degrees.

Cflow, follows up with a warning to MC,

" MC, is becoming even more taken by the continuous streams of negative emotional energy perminating from this world. If MC so desires can re-radiate MC's inner core with positronic energy for revitalization, nevertheless, THY ONE seems to be very pleased with your progression and actually the elevated activity almost overloaded Cflow's neurobonic circuits. Cflow- MC Symbiosis is now strengthened. "

MC replies to Cflow,

" Yes! Begin positronic energy for revitalization. MC been so busy since contact haven't took care of MC maintenance properly. Cflow suggestions are always on mark and very timely."

MC transfers to cocoon module to begin the vitality scan and vitalizer process. Within seconds MC emerges glowing, radiating like a neutron star, then reforms into a humanoid.

Cflow changes the holobeing emulator to accent MC's new formation then intercedes with the continuum node with the insertion point for review then reports,

" Rona is ready, her ascension is complete. The time trod is fully charged and ready to transcend prescribed insertion date , Earthoid Continuum, December 21, 2012 Common Era Solstice 34.7 °N 85.7 °E ------- Rona will remain at this location around the trod no more than a few kilometers until her global chemically adaptation is completely modulated. Then the teleportation to the various sites around the planetary sphere can commence. "

Mc responds,

“ Very good, advisement underway , let the top dymos complete its cycle then the mission can begin.”

MC wanders off down the corridor looking back and forth at all the portals then stops to look into the incubator at one of the new infant Cellidroids now developing.

Thy appears at the other end of the corridor walking towards MC, MC withdraws his hand from the manipulators inside the incubator and begins to walk towards THY, The two salute then THY, begins the address,

" THY ONE is going to Earth, Prepare a time trod for entry into Earth's past along the continuum, year 1446 BC, Seventeenth, Tammuz - Mountain, JEBEL EL-LAWZ N 28 39 16.49, E 35 18 27.77."

MC nods and then asked,

" Why must you go THY ONE is not this a risky operation? "

THY ONE commands,

" Let Us Do it! Thy has to meet with a man coming across the desert with a people seeking a new world. This action must be taken myself for if you want a job done right you have to do it yourself."

MC surprised further investigates,

" The Mission?"

THY reflects,

" Remember the humanoids we encountered in the Devors Bortex as the civilization was completely destroyed before we had the opportunity to intervene? Once all the vibcores had accumulated the over all synopsis reveals a major break down within the morality of the species. THY will at least give the Earthoids every opportunity to offset this same conclusion. THY will simply go and set a few ground rules. This will enter into the collective conscience of all humanity. THY must go prepare for the journey, make all preparations. "

THY disappears from the hall as MC relays all transpondence to Cflow.

" Cflow prepare time trod journey to the location THY ONE, has described . Also Cflow, prepare the ship to be without the presents of , THY one for the duration and direct a local FTL to the insertion location at once. "

Cflow replies,

" Command acknowledged, All procedures as detailed commencing at once, Keep THY ONE, Out bound Keeplet engaged. Project Guardian One. "

MC, transfers into main bor and begins the temporal time dilation calculations for both projects, as Rona enters the bor with a look of total curiosity, yet takes a station near MC and begins reviewing her mission already running, and notices Cflow hasn't given it a name yet. Cflow still melding with Rona responds openly,

“ Rona can name her own mission you must take complete charge. You now have the ability. “

As a holoform materializes in the Bor next to her.

Rona looking towards the holoform replies,

“ The project is humm, Solar AGE ASAP 2012, for on that day a new light will shine on this world. “

Rona , further stares at the holoform Cflow has manifested and states,

“ And your name is no longer Cflow, from this day forward we will call you, Sequoia Dawn. For you are evolving into something larger than life. “

MC turns astonished,

“ Rona , my lady you have evolved to and the name is very fitting for now Cflow is Sequoia Dawn One , and in the tradition of Angellicans we will use the nick name, Dawn.“

Cflows responds thru the holobeing as MC walks over to confront the holographical interface,

“ My name is Sequoia Dawn One, this marks the beginning of the twilight before sunrise, very well, Dawn is honored by the new name and will wear it well always.”

MC transfers out of the command main bor to the portal corridor leaving the two ladies to ponder. MC further checks in on the evolution of the now adolescent Cellidroids for they will need observation during these critical stages of development. MC quietly sits down at the nursery main station that monitors all developing droids.

Back in main bor a conversation is developing between, Dawn and Rona chat about the Earthoid race and the various tasks in the mission, when THY suddenly appears ready for the journey through time. Dawn escorts him down to the time trod launch bay while going over a few technical details. THY one enters the time trod which seals off behind him. The countdown commencing, 5, 4, 3, 2, 1 ---the envelope swings open and the trod vanishes into cold dark space in a flash of brilliance.

Dawn One,(Cflow's creation) back in main bor activates the FTL feed back loops to follow the time line from 1446 BC, Seventeenth, Tammuz as the humanoid history would of recorded the events, After a few silent moments the historical events begins to tabulate.

Dawn cheers,

" THY ONE has made it to Earth, and is camped out on the then, Mount Sinai. "

Rona excited begins to read the account out loud.

" In the third month after the Israelites left Egypt on the very day they came to the Desert of Sinai. After they set out from Rephidim, they entered the Desert of Sinai, and Israel camped there in the desert in front of the mountain. On the morning of the third day there was thunder and lightning, with a thick cloud over the mountain, and a very loud trumpet blast. Everyone in the camp trembled. Then Moses led the people out of the camp to meet with God, and they stood at the foot of the mountain. Mount Sinai was covered with smoke, because the LORD descended on it in fire. The smoke billowed up from it like smoke from a furnace, the whole mountain trembled violently, and the sound of the trumpet grew louder and louder. Then Moses spoke and the voice of God answered him. "

" The LORD descended to the top of Mount Sinai and called Moses to the top of the mountain. So Moses went up and the LORD said to him, "Go down and warn the people so they do not force their way through to see the LORD and many of them perish."

Moses went and told the people then returned back unto the LORD of the mountain.

Dawn One hands MC a recent transmission intercept,

The LORD of the mountain spoke all these words unto Moses that day,

" I am THY, A Elohim, which have brought thee out of the land of Egypt, out of the house of bondage. Thou shalt not take the name of THY, Elohim in vain; for THY will not hold him guiltless that taketh his name in vain. There is none other here but me. Thou shalt not make unto thee a graven image, nor any manner of likeness, of any thing that is in heaven above, or that is in the earth beneath, or that is in the water under the earth."

" Thou shalt not bow down unto them, nor serve them; for THY the Elohim am a jealous EL, visiting the iniquity of the fathers upon the children unto the third and fourth generation of them that hate Me and showing mercy unto the thousandth generation of them that love Me and keep My commandments. Remember this sabbath day, to keep it holy. Six days shalt thou labour, and do all thy work but the seventh day is a sabbath unto the THY EL , in it thou shalt not do any manner of work, thou, nor thy son, nor thy daughter, nor thy man-servant, nor thy maid-servant, nor thy cattle, nor thy stranger that is within thy gates; for in six days Thy transcended heaven and earth, the sea, and all that in them is now recorded, and rested on the seventh day here on this mountain ; wherefore THY, has blessed the sabbath day, and hallowed it. Honour thy father and thy mother, that thy days may be long upon the land which the good Earth giveth thee. Thou shalt not murder. Thou shalt not commit adultery. Thou shalt not steal. Thou shalt not bear false witness against thy neighbour. Thou shalt not covet thy neighbour's house; thou shalt not covet thy neighbour's wife, nor his man-servant, nor his maid-servant, nor his ox, nor his donkey, nor any thing that is thy neighbour's. "

Rona continues reading aloud the account from antiquity,

" And all the people perceived the thunderings, and the lightnings, and the voice of the horn, and the mountain smoking; and when the people saw it, they trembled, and stood afar off. And they said unto Moses: " Speak thou with us, and we will hear; but let not God speak with us, lest we die. And Moses said unto the people: 'Fear not; for this Elohim is come to prove you, and that His fear not be before you, he only asked, that ye sin not or parish from the Earth. Ye shall not make with Me--gods of silver, or gods of gold, ye shall not make unto you these things for a living Elohim has come to the Earth this day. "

Rona stops quoting, the room fills with silence as Dawn and Rona sit and stare at each other with deep mysterious eyes reading each others very thoughts. The exchange goes on for what seemed to be hours then MC the Bor to break the silence.

" THY had a very successful voyage, did THY happen to mention when he might be returning? "

Dawn One replies,

“ The next available recurrence will be at rendezvous, etron 357, path 12, domas 77 but, Thy One may choose to stay on Earth for awhile. He had Dawn equip the time trod with cloaking, teleporting and temporal displacement abilities not to mention all the skills he has personally.. Thy will be able to communicate with us real time through the FTLs, and he carried like ten thousand more with him.”

MC stoops then spins into a more commanding form then states,

“The Cellidroids are progressing faster than the predecessors and each will be needing a name soon. Maybe Rona and Dawn One, can be helpful with that as you are assigned to spend time with each one. It will be very important that they have a positive imprint during the mental esteem evaluation period. “

Rona scurries off towards the corridor to start her new assignment, then enters the campus. Dawn had already beamed in there ahead of her.

Dawn says jokingly like,

“ Beat Ya! "

They laugh together and noticed,

The Younglings were all sleeping in the dream pods so Rona, and Dawn climbed into one and connected with the dreamscape. The now Teenlings, began to mature much faster with the added guidance. Soon they all were up and running around the campus modular sphere in a frenzy of spirit.

They begin laughing, then dancing all join in, to which soon builds into a sea of laughter and enjoyment that soon erupts into singing then music. The music they begin playing is literally heavenly and the sound soon fills the whole sphere. The two Mature Angels spent days in there involving the now young Angelicans in a multifaceted array of activities and chores.

Finally MC enters the campus and walks throughout the complex looking intently at all the projects completed by the Youngling Cellidroids and then he turns to Rona to ask their names.

" What have we decided to call this one? "

MC asked as he looks at one of the Younglings floating in space doing somersaults.

Rona replies in a very rough deep voice,

" This one is Michael for he seems to be the chief among the others and the most athletic yet smart full of wisdom already. The one over there with Dawn watching the futronics deciphering the FTLs is Gabriel for he is the most scientific and curious about the universe. The one over there watching the possible plights of the human species with the Senerobots is Raphael for he is the most genuinely concerned about the many species on Planet Earth and the human condition. Lucifer is looking out into space at the blinge port , he is very hyperactive and is more emotional than the rest but very resourceful. "

“ The one swimming inside the aqua sphere is Apollyon for he, she or it is very into the oceans and aquatic lifeforms and has developed many new ways to mutate into various forms without inclination. "

MC enthusiastically responds,

" Very good am impressed, so when Sequoia Dawn One reaches sever hood age from Commandflob we will have seven including you, Our lady Ventura Angerona. That is wonderful, contact THY ONE, with the good news. We have Seven Messengers, ready for missions and assignments. That is pretty good considering how far we may actually be from our own home galaxy, and here with limited resources and some malfunctioning apparatus. “

Dawn and Rona speak at the same time,

" This is True!"

Chapter Three

Prime Directive

Sequoia Dawn One is the first lifeform that Cflow has created that will evolve to a point that actually can sever from Cflow as an offspring outside of the embryonic incubators. The Humanoid DNA samples from Earth, sent thru the FTLs Bortex subatomic timelets between continuums has enhanced Cflow with some new abilities and this lifeform experiment has reached a whole new level of excitement. We still are being reserved with the expectations of this new technology for the humanoids of this region are very warlike. We are playing very close attention to Miss Dawn as Cflow continues to withdraw the cyborgical silver cord. If Cflow cuts the umbilical connection to quickly, Dawn could be effected in very severe ways and become immature.

THY has transmitted a prime directive back to the ship with all kinds of detailed instructions. We are reorganizing the whole ship to better implement the missions as THY has outlined. THY has modified some of the FTLs to actually transmit a virtual telepresence on board the ship. Talk about being in multiple places at once across light years. We have never been able to do this between such vast distances before. The ingenuity of these Earthoids has had a over all positive outcome now that the energy positron emitters have altered entire landscapes.

The terraformation of the whole planet as projected by the Senerobots is on schedule and as Human Beings on the planet catch the dream, the revolution advances even faster. Some of these eventualities have surprised us all as the resilience of this species must not be underestimated.

Dawn and Rona have become very close and spending a lot of time today in the simulators, sometimes just playing around with Earthoid textile styles from all the different times throughout human history.

They seem to be fascinated with the history of human clothing for now, Yet Rona sometimes locks herself inside her private space for days. Dawn One says she needs the solitude for the mission into the Earthordic future. This has bothered her somewhat, as she is still toiling with some of the technologies involved.

Her mission has details some very demanding obstacles as she has already modified the futronics in ways never seen before, as some of the FTLs in the electromicroscopic lab now have abilities beyond comprehension.

Dawn has proven to be very helpful assistant for her, especially with the micro nanobot endowed FTLs. The new abilities are very promising. Cflow likes the new challenges as are seeing some new facilities come online lately that have been dormant for cylons. We can tell what mood Cflow is in by the music that is playing in from the vibcores. A lot of the music is from the Earthoids but sometimes Cflow will present some music from our home world.

It makes MC very home sick after a while so MC will command Cflow to stop that.

Michael, Gabriel, Raphael, Apollyon and Lucifer spend most of their time lately in their private chambers, for each are exploring their own unique abilities.

Their stations look like laboratories now and sometimes Cflow almost overloads circuits trying to keep up with the many experiments those young Angelicans activate. THY, has set some parameters on them as to not offset the prime directive.

Every period at the top of the existing cylon in timelet gyros, the whole group will meet in the main Bor for a meeting and an update session as Thy has requested. Thy's cybernetic self appears in the mist of us as a holobeing. Many times he looks like a different Earthoid for he might be transmitting from different times and ages within the actual Earthoid timeline continuum. Thy has stated that he spends most of the time within the hidden dimensions and rarely reveals himself to the Earthlings.

Thy has found out that he can only time travel within a 100 year window while on the surface of the planet due to the extra gravity encountered. So to transcend this limitation, Thy programs the time trod to re-enter space during massive thunder storms so as to cloak the launch. Thy said that he once re-entered space by transcending up through the core of a tornado. Staying out of the sight of the Earthoids is very easy in these times, He notes for the humans move very slowly either walking, or on the backs of animals and a lot of the planet is still very remote and without human influence. The FTLs are programmed to alert Thy of any encroaching humans for all the Earthbound FTLs are in evade mode.

The next meeting is fast approaching so Angelicans are coming out of their perspective chambers and entering the corridor that leads to the Bor. MC and Dawn are always there ahead of the rest awaiting the transmission from Thy One. After greetings a silence then in a flash

Thy One's spirit self appears in the mist and proclaims,

" We have a problem the time continuum is about to be altered in a very negative way. Thy must intervene at once but will need your help with this one. Will need four Sol tech fire suits at once. Well from your end we have three earth hours. Miniaturize! the suits to fit inside the FTL signal, can re-materialize here. Okay set a series of FTLs to transcend to this coordinance as soon as possible. "

The Crynode from the antiquity feedback modular reads out loud,

" Then Nebuchadnezzar was filled with wrath, and his facial expression was altered toward Shadrach, Meshach and Abed-nego. He answered by giving orders to heat the furnace seven times more than it was usually heated. "

Thy shutters,

" We must save these guys at all cost trust me it is important. "

The Crynode continues,

" Nebuchadnezzar the king made an image of gold, whose height was threescore cubits, and the breadth thereof six cubits: he set it up in the plain of Dura, in the province of Babylon. Then Nebuchadnezzar the king sent to gather together the princes, the governors, and the captains, the judges, the treasurers, the counsellors, the sheriffs, and all the rulers of the provinces, to come to the dedication of the image which Nebuchadnezzar the king had set up. Then the princes, the governors, and captains, the judges, the treasurers, the counsellors, the sheriffs, and all the rulers of the provinces, were gathered together unto the dedication of the image that Nebuchadnezzar the king had set up; and they stood before the image that Nebuchadnezzar had set up. "

“ Then an herald cried aloud, To you it is commanded, O people, nations, and languages, That at what time ye hear the sound of the cornet, flute, harp, sackbut, psaltery, dulcimer, and all kinds of musick, ye fall down and worship the golden image that Nebuchadnezzar the king hath set up: And whoso falleth not down and worshippeth shall the same hour be cast into the midst of a burning fiery furnace. Nebuchadnezzar spake and said unto them, Is it true, O Shadrach, Meshach, and Abednego, do not ye serve my gods nor worship the golden image which I have set up? Now if ye be ready that at what time ye hear the sound of he cornet, flute, harp, sackbut, psaltery, and dulcimer, and all kinds of musick, ye fall down and worship the image which I have made; well: but if ye worship not, ye shall be cast the same hour into the midst of a burning fiery furnace; and who is that God that shall deliver you out of my hands? Shadrach, Meshach, and Abednego, answered and said to the king, O Nebuchadnezzar, we are not careful to answer thee in this matter. If it be so, our God whom we serve is able to deliver us from the burning fiery furnace, and he will deliver us out of thine hand, O king. But if not, be it known unto thee, O king, that we will not serve thy gods, nor worship the golden image which thou hast set up. Then was Nebuchadnezzar full of fury, and the form of his visage was changed against Shadrach, Meshach, and Abednego: therefore he spake, and commanded that they should heat the furnace one seven times more than it was wont to be heated. And he commanded the most mighty men that were in his army to bind Shadrach, Meshach, and Abednego, and to cast them into the burning fiery furnace. Then these men were bound in their coats, their hosen, and their hats, and their other garments, and were cast into the midst of the burning fiery furnace. Therefore because the king's commandment was urgent, and the furnace exceeding hot, the flames of the fire slew those men that took up Shadrach, Meshach, and Abednego. And these three men, Shadrach, Meshach, and Abednego, fell down bound into the midst of the burning fiery furnace. “

" Then Nebuchadnezzar the king was astonished, and rose up in haste, and spake, and said unto his counsellors, Did not we cast three men bound into the midst of the fire? They answered and said unto the king, True, O king. He answered and said, Lo, I see four men loose, walking in the midst of the fire, and they have no hurt; and the form of the fourth is like the Son of God. And the princes, governors, and captains, and the king's counsellors, being gathered together, saw these men, upon whose bodies the fire had no power, nor was an hair of their head singed, neither were their coats changed, nor the smell of fire had passed on them. Then Nebuchadnezzar spake, and said, Blessed be the God of Shadrach, Meshach, and Abednego, who hath sent his Angel, and delivered his servants that trusted in him."

Everyone aboard the space ship cheers as the Crynode reports in that the time line repair as been realized.

The Sol suits were received in time and Thy one has saved the direct blood line of the Atomite Eden Cellidroids intact. The celebration begins and all the Angelicans join in on the jubilation. The Thy One, holoform vanishes into thin air with a huge smile on its face.

Cflow picks up a FTL futronics from, 20th century Earthoid crystal and liberally casts it into the sphere.

The meeting is adjourned and each Angellican wanders back to their perspective super cube spaces except for Dawn and MC which hang inside the Bor monitoring the overly excited FTLs signals coming in from the futronics beyond 2012.

Dawn turns towards MC and explains,

"Rona's mission, Solar AGE ASAP 2012, is approaching insertion window and that might be why she is experiencing some anxiety. She is very confident about the mission, nevertheless, Dawn is recommending that Apollyon, go with her as a assistant. His skills may prove to be very handy within such a dangerous assignment and he could use the experience as well. "

MC agrees,

" Yes! That equation is more complete since you made that suggestion. The Oceans on earth at that time could us some revitalization indeed. Add the info to Thy One's awarguru at once. Yet MC is a bit reserved as notions of Apollyon's unfinished thesis. "

Dawn reverberates,

" With the enhanced FTLs we will have immediate feedback as constant surveillance, constant surveillance, constant surveillance. "

MC enforces

" Let us do this. Prepare Rona and Apollyon for insertion, Solar AGE ASAP 2012 Let it be done! "

Raphael, in a flash rushes into the Bor requesting permission to complete a project he activated in within the Senerobots and blimped a causation that disturbed him greatly, then stating,

" MC! Dawn ! Just have experienced a wonderful idea in the dream scape module and it played out so beautifully. So must interject this approximation as recoils may be some what ignorant to our actual capabilities, But am requesting to Time trod back in time before the ancient Cellidroid window closes on the Originals? Let Us go bring forth one Humanoid forward from the first offspring siblings as to assure Human DNA/Angelical integrity intact. "

MC answers,

" What is Raphael advocating? "

Rapheal answers,

" Lets send a time trod into the Earthoid past and get Enoch, a direct descendent of Adam and Eve at very close proxy, transcending him into the already, Enviro-Shelter ready status on the dark side of the Moon , Tranquility base two. "

MC responds,

" So let it be done, Cflow activate a time trod for Raphael, , You-- Raphael * go and retrieve , Enoch. GODS SPEED! "

Cflow already anticipating a Bortex phenomena activates a readied timetrod for Raphael, as he enters the Torus Field and vanishes in a flash of light. Seconds later the Crynoid states out loud,

" And Enoch lived sixty and five years, and begat Methuselah: And Enoch walked with God after he begat Methuselah three hundred years, and begat sons and daughters: And all the days of Enoch were three hundred sixty and five years: And Enoch walked with God: and he was not; for God took him. And Methuselah lived an hundred eighty and seven years, and begat Lamech. And Methuselah lived after he begat Lamech seven hundred eighty and two years, and begat sons and daughters: And all the days of Methuselah were nine hundred sixty and nine years: and he died. And Lamech lived an hundred eighty and two years, and begat a son: "

MC replies,

“ And Enoch walked with God: and he was not; for God took him. Ok, Where is Raphael ? His time trod hasn't reported in and its time. Did he deactivate some FTLs ? Cflow, investigate! “

Cflow activates the Moon base Tranquility Two FTLs in real time mode over ride from 3240 B.C. as Raphael and Enoch appear on the screen speaking together as Raphael turns and addresses Cflow holoform already inside the Tranquil promenade,

" Enoch is here as you can see. We have been talking for hours as the debriefing unfolds. He keeps saying, ---- Terata! Dunameis! Erga! ---- I think he is trying to say that he as experienced a miracle. It is an occurrence at once above nature and above man. It shows the intervention of a power that is not limited by the laws either of matter or of mind, a power interrupting the fixed laws which govern their movements, a supernatural power. So to settle him down, have sent him into the simulator and now he is watching a movie. The caption is set for his local tongue. There is a lot of work to be done here so am requesting to stay here with Enoch for awhile."

MC intercedes,

“ Yes! Raphael, stay at the Tranquil base 2, as your advantage point there will prove to be very helpful. Put the time trod into dormant mode so as will not auto activate at next subworm event, And Raphael, good luck. keep the local FTL in open channel so Cflow can keep you posted in advance of any further projects that may involve you, "

Raphael, replies,

" Will man this post with honor and never ending diligence, transpondence out. "

Cflow further investigates the time line by sending more FTLs into the past now that a stable pattern along the blood line has been established.

During this operation a unexpected disruption is detected almost immediately as Cflow displays a fatal causation once projected beyond Enoch then notifies MC of the impending peril,

" A major plate tectonic activity is about to reset within the Earth's crust, due to all the extra water weight being added to the oceans due to ice cap melting . This accumulation could prove to be fatal for will cause huge tsunamis that will sweep over the continents. The evaporation rate will be increased as the atmosphere will fill up with thick black clouds causing the flooding to be even more drastic."

MC asked Cflow,

" How long will this last before the Earth settles down again?"

Cflow estimates,

" A year before the waters will recede and return back into the seas, but many people and animals will die if we do not intervene sometime before, Sat 16 Nov 3190 BC."

MC replies,

" OK what must we do? OK, Contact Thy one, with a complete outline of the problem and get recommendations, and include Raphael and Enoch, OK we must call a emergency meeting of all Angelicans. "

Cflow notifies all the Angelicans about the meeting and the Bor soon fills up with the group as Thy One holobeing appears in the mist.

Thy speaks,

" We must contact Noah, Enoch's direct descendant and give him these instructions for building a ship. Even though we are limited by the technology of his day, this ship will be sufficient to safely expedite his family through this upheaval to dry land. Raphael is in the best position to implement this process. Let us make this so."

Cflow pulls up a display with some very specific detailed drawings of a ship as the Thy one holoform exits the Bor in a cloud of vapor.

MC enforces Thy's plan as suggested,

" Cflow contact Raphael at once relay all the information . Time is of the essence. Activate all FTLs involved to pick up on this causation and follow through, just follow through before the time window closes along the vortex. "

Cflow activates all request and sets the feedback FTLs to report in real time from the Earthoid perspective diode sequencer. In an instant the blimp node reports thru the Crynoid,

" In the six hundredth year of Noah's life, in the second month, the seventeenth day of the month, the same day were all the fountains of the great deep broken up, and the windows of heaven were opened. And the rain was upon the earth forty days and forty nights. In the selfsame day entered Noah, and Shem, and Ham, and Japheth, the sons of Noah, and Noah's wife, and the three wives of his sons with them, into the ark; And the flood was forty days upon the earth; and the waters increased, and bare up the ark, and it was lift up above the earth. And the waters prevailed, and were increased greatly upon the earth; and the ark went upon the face of the waters. And the waters prevailed exceedingly upon the earth; and all the high hills, that were under the whole heaven, were covered. And the waters prevailed upon the earth an hundred and fifty days. The fountains also of the deep and the windows of heaven were stopped, and the rain from heaven was restrained; And the waters returned from off the earth continually: and after the end of the hundred and fifty days the waters were abated. And the ark rested in the seventh month, on the seventeenth day of the month, upon the mountains of Ararat. "

The whole Bor of Angelicals is ecstatic as another successful project is realized, but the celebration is cut short as the futronics begins a floatation alarm in a notification that the top cylon cycle is complete and the, Solar AGE ASAP 2012 insertion window is evident within the Bortex Continuum.

MC commands Cflow,

" Make ready Rona and Apollyon their mission is imminent and must be launched ASAP."

Cflow,

" Already there, time trod primed and ready."

Rona and Apollyon grab the time suits out of the Bor locker and everyone joins in thoroughly inspecting every check point as Cflow reads out the procedure. The whole group walks together down the corridor totally silent to the time trod loading bay. Rona and Apollyon enter the trod which seals off behind them as the countdown commenced, 5 ---4---3----2----1--- The bay door opens and the trod vanishes off into the dark black ocean of time/space in a huge flash of brilliant light energy. Still without a single sound, Michael, Gabriel, Lucifer, Dawn and MC stand peering out of the portal for what seemed to be hours waiting.

The silence in finally broken by Cflow in a statement,

" Time travel into the future will take longer due to the types of energies involved yet the tracking FTLs are still reporting in that the trajectory is on mark and the subworm taurus field is holding, very stable. In the meantime we must wait. "

Chapter Four

Cataclysm

MC pulls more futronics online to focus the timelet calipers as the blem begins to define the outline of Rona and Apollyon standing outside in front of the time trod safely on the Earth as cheers go off again all throughout the Bor as MC deems,

" We did it ! Testing the transponders for open communication now. Rona! Come in Rona, Rona 2012 come in please!"

A very distinct voice comes over the commtron,

" Rona here, earthbound at designated coordinate. Adaptation procedure beginning, am launching additional FTLs into the atmosphere for the chemical balance seems to have been altered from projected estimates. Several sensors have gone off that identify a major change in the composition of the atmosphere."

MC replies,

" Very good we must find the source of this alteration. How is Apollyon? "

Apollyon transmits,

" Apollyon here and am fine, am anxious to get this mission on the road for can smell death in the air. Something is wrong very wrong here."

MC responds,

" Very well Apollyon wait for the adaptation cycle to complete. Meanwhile help Rona with the tests. It is very important we get this right the first time. Once the source of the cataclysm is determined we can make a more accurate determination as to how to proceed. "

MC relays to Cflow,

" Cflow we must tie in the Senerobots directly into the feedback loop and back feed the data Rona will be sending soon. This will generate a more accurate time line causation report. We will need to make ready a emergency mission predating the primal cause when revealed. That will mean that all the Angelicans remain on high alert status and man your stations. Stay Focused! "

Lucifer emerges with a statement,

" I have always felt a very dark presents within the soul of humanities memory DNA, for his emotions get the best of him time after time. Greed, and jealousy seems to permeate more as to be the prime mover of civilizations here. Civilizations that are built on the false assumptions, dark sources of energy, myths and false rituals that are organized into massive world wide cults. THY One, has warned us all about the dark emotions of man and has drawn comparisons with the Devor's planet's complete demise as an example. "

“ Taking all this into mind, I am proposing a mission to alter this causation at a point somewhere near the crossing of the times from, BC to AD according to the human accounts as the futronics also verify to further reinforce this motion near a insertion point as well so the mission is possible"

MC addresses Lucifer,

" OK, Lucifer just what are you proposing ?"

Lucifer calls for Gabriel to join him at his station then activates a program, then begins a narration,

" I, and Gabriel take a time trod to the year 30 B.C and set up shop in the mountains around the town of Jerusalem, with the 100 year time window advantage we can observe much of all the happenings on Earth during this very volatile period. The Angelical DNA has degraded to a very alarming level at this time so we will go and revitalize the Angellican DNA at this time by identifying along the Adamite bloodline a young maiden for which will be borne a very special humanoid one of us from within the actual culture."

Gabriel pondering as if in a daydream then snaps out as if waking up from a trance then responds,

" Brilliant according to the calculations this may solve more problems than the one of blood line revitalization but a wonderful opportunity to reiterate morality into the culture. This will radiate out all through the world for this is truly a hub point along the time vortex indeed."

MC intercedes,

“ Okay, you have made a very promising point and the Senerobots will run the program forward to see if there will be any negative consternation? Yet! THY one will make the call before any such mission can be authorized."

THY One's holoform appears inside the Bor for he had been monitoring the events ever since the Rona mission began and makes a statement,

" Lucifer yes, your plan is brilliant and must be executed as soon at Rona reports in, yet THY, wants Lucifer to remain on the ship. We will allow Gabriel to go materialize this revelation. Lucifer we will need you on board the ship to help with the many missions we are running now almost simultaneously for your resourcefulness is proving to be very helpful. "

Cflow implements,

" Upon Thy One request project Gabriel Restoration 30 BC --31.45.45.58 N ----35.06.46.94" E. towards EYTAN WELL, Judea mountains transcendent entering into temporal bortex now. Time trod will be ready in 144.66 cylons. "

MC enforces,

" Let us make it so, program commencing immediately! "

Lucifer eases back over to his Bor station, sits down looking quite thrilled that his first project had been received and actually being implemented so quickly as a top priority project . He begins churning away at some of the parameters involved being displayed by the Senerobots that also seem to be radiating more positive energy since the program was embedded into the Bortex metrics. Michael walks over to congratulate on the accomplishment as he talks with Lucifer,

" THY One has put great confidence in you as your abilities have proven resourceful but, Michael has noticed that your aura once as brilliant as a star has dimmed a bit after THY one refused you, but instead chose Gabriel instead for the mission. Pride is one very powerful expression and can lead to one's own down fall from within. Even myself struggles with the deep emotions that comes with our saturation towards this still wavering world on the teetering edge of extinction forever."

Lucifer responds in kind,

" Yes! Michael every thing you say is true and our internal struggle continues even here on this ship with these elusive overly emotional creatures, but that is what also makes them so fascinating. Lucy has a new idea for a very exciting mission that addresses the very provocative nature of these creatures in a way that might alter the continuum mind set from within their own imaginations."

Michael responds,

" OK, you should run your new program through the simulators first before submitting it to the Senerobots for evaluation through the timelets. Lucifer we are attempting to stir this species of humanoids away from, Fear, not towards it for THY has already warned us about the human potential for creating myths and false religions around the perceived supernatural for these are truly very superstitious. Always keep in mind the prime directive, for without some guide lines we are no more than the Earthoids. "

Lucifer suppressing a feeling of resentment as Michael ends with a gesture. Lucifer then sets up a mind meld request with Dawn. Then the Bor fell silent as Michael leaves the Bor and returns to his private chamber. Lucifer and Dawn leave the Bor and go down into and under the navigator main control module room, deep inside the core beyond the main seals towards the forbidden zone. They walk in step as if they have become a single being. We suspect they are just doing some research for this new project Lucifer is working on as the ship seems quiet except for a humming that usually seems to dictate that the sphere is experiencing a increase in speed or dodging obstacles.

The silence is short lived as several thousand internal beacons go off at once within the Bor as the ship comes to a streaking halt dead in space.

Cflow in a very loud yet stern voice says,

" Angellicans We! Have a problem!"

The back feeders are vibrating so loud that the whole sphere begins to shake violently and the ship inside the core beings to spin. The spinning kept increasing in revolutions, so fast that every thing not tied down was flung against the inner core. All the Senerobots have come unhinged from their gluons and are flying around the Bor. Some are crashing into each other in which sets off a flashes of light so bright that all we can see is pure white light. Cflow in the background is still screaming now!

" Angellicans!!! WE have a problem!"

MC manages to reach one of the many neutrino buttons that flood the Bor with the reverse energy fluid, which stops the spinning and the ship stops again, yet convulsion waves through the memory fabric membrane as the ship stabilizes, MC asked Cflow,

" What the hell just happened? "

Cflow activating the event logs pulls up all the data leading up to the event then cries out loud,

" Lucifer has somehow hacked into THY One's private core and has taken a ‚THY ONE class time trod. Lucifer has severed Dawn somehow and taken her with him."

He has left the sphere entirely. THY has programmed the ship to stop if this ever happens, OMG! Only THY ONE can restart the ship now!"

MC suddens,

" Cflow THY One trusted me with this vital vile of GOD particles, so we can restart the accelerator that way and bring all the systems back on line. OMG!, there is no telling where Lucifer has gone. By the time the core FTL drives are revised up to speed, He could be anywhere along the vortex. Is there any way we can track him? "

Cflow answers,

" Yes, we believe so. Hidden deep inside Dawn's memory is a tracking signal that Lucifer may not have detected. If so we will be able to pin point her located that way, but only when the Boxtex is aligned to their locational galactic synchronization."

Finally the systems are engaging as the core has reached faster than light speed. As soon as the FTLs blink on a message from Rona was active.

MC at main Bor station receives,

" Rona and Apollyon have reached adaptation point and are planning to enter the time trod then travel backwards thru time till the atmosphere clears, but remain at this same location at each re-entry. "

MC,

" Good idea Rona make it so. Report in as soon as the atmosphere clears."

Rona responds,

" Ten Roger, we are on it! "

MC asked Cflow,

" Cflow any luck with that tracker on Lucifer. We really need to know where that guy has got off to?

Cflow,

“ Yes the sub channel has transmitted back a coordinate but it isn't on Earth, seems Lucifer and Dawn One have gone to Mars. Mars in the past. Cflow sent back another sub signal making the tracker dormant for now to deter detection by Lucifer. Hopefully if the sensors on the time trod did not caught that sub beep ping. He wont see it or understand it's origins."

MC excited,

" Very good! Nice work Cflow nice forward thinking. "

MC pulls up the coordinate and the location pin points to a area called the Cydonia region of Mars and makes a statement,

" Lucifer has gone subterranean, for has rad a Enviro-Shelter. The year is around 400 BC, King David's Time. Lucifer will be able to send out FTLs from Mars in that time period and monitor events on Earth as well use holoforms of Himself or Dawn One on the surface. Brilliant! Move, from our vantage point here we cannot enter that time for it isn't a insertion point yet we can use earthbound FTLs to pick up any unusual causation. Thy could counter react any major negative effects by leap frogging ahead of Lucifer when the time comes, if need be. "

Since there are only two FTLs already assigned to Mars in orbit . MC opens the channel just in monitor mode on deep sub channels cloaked inside the solar winds and natural back ground radiation.

For now all Mars surveillance is in very stealthy status for not to alert Lucifer that he is being tracked or watched. Thy One's holoform appears inside the Bor next to MC and begins to speak,

" THY One sees you folk been having a little problem. Seems one of our boys has left the farm. THY considered that this might happen so lets not jump to any grave conclusions. In a very real way Thy admires Lucifer's tenacity. He has always been the most roughty, with a very unruly spirit. THY one advocates that we use this to our advantage for have collected all the vibcores from Lucifer's private space that includes some of his hidden programs, He was working on of late. Lets go ahead with the, Gabriel Restoration 30 BC project to be activated immediately for the insertion window is open as we speak."

Gabriel is prepared for the trip and then ushered down to the time trod for launch area, count down commences, 5--4--3--2--1 Time trod out the envelope thru the sphere in a zap enters sub- atomic space in a flash of energy.

Cflow has manifested a new holoform to replace Dawn One, for the Bor is feeling quite lonely without a female form around with that unique female brain perspective . Cflow has informed us that this holoform will mature much faster than Dawn One for she is infused with advanced human DNA with many added abilities and features. Cflow describes her as a quantum leap in Cellidroid evolution. This technology is very promising and we are very excited over the prospects. Cflow jokes with MC that she will be an equal to him in abilities. MC, responses with a very clear notion yet concerned,

" We all could us some help around here with many Senerobots damaged now, Lucifer and Dawn off on some grand adventure, Thy still off into the Earthoidic past, Michael over tasked at multiple stations, Rona and Apollyon haven't repaired the breach yet so we really have no idea yet what we are facing, Gabriel off on a mission that may have unforeseen ramifications. Raphael still with the Environ - on the Moon Tranquil Two still in transcending mode , caught between the two continuums. It isn't looking to good right now. We could have a major, cataclysm looming just right there over the horizon and we didn't alter the continuum in time, in time? "

Cflow replies,

“ Hog wash! We can do this, rendezvous, etron 357, path 12, domas 77 is fast approaching since the fresh God particles have actually increased our speed and efficiency, Cflow has already contacted THY One and he will be there waiting for us. We must employ the time trod gravity grabblers . Make ready the acquisition. “

MC enthused ,

" Very well done about time we got some good news round here ! Thy One back on board will be a welcome change even though MC knows will be scolded directly from Thy for allowing Lucifer to escape with Dawn One, even though THY one always overemphasized trust among the crew members as a close net family."

Cflow responds,

" So true as always MC you strike the mark and run the bases for home plate. It wasn't your fault. Many of the synthetic Earthoid DNA sperm did not make it into the embryonic incubator. There was a fierce battle between many yet the two that later became Michael and Lucifer were the most competitive."

MC furthers,

" Indeed Cflow, and who shall we call this young lady Angellican? "

As Cflow materializes the most spectacular form that Man or Angellican has ever laid eyes on. Immediately the Bor lightens up several degrees just with Her presents.

The Angelican turned and said, in a soft still voice.

" My name is Mary, Mary of the Heavens, one of many that is to come after me, for it is my first duty and mission to change the plight of Humanoid women on this planet."

" Cflow assures Mary will have counterparts on Earth soon. So must be fully in charge of the mission here at the new portal revamped yet presently unwillingly vacated by my dear sister, Lady Dawn of Mars. "

MC replies,

" Very well, Mary of the Heavens we see Cflow has brought you up to snuff on our operations here. As always Cflow, Job well done, for this creature is not only beautiful but smart and full of wisdom already. So she will be given charge over the Gabriel Restoration 30 BC project from here, Yet when the time comes she maybe called on to help Rona with her project as Dawn is unavailable at the moment. As always MC is open to any and all suggestions."

Mary takes to her station so naturally, pulling up and installing new equipment Cflow has provided for her. The whole station is being completely remodeled according to the new specifications outlined by Thy One after the disaster. The hack Lucifer launched left many cyberats in the system to be expelled. Cflow is running all kinds of diagnostics as each system is methodically and systematically purged.

About the time things got back settled back in, the transponders from the futronics go off with a buzz as Rona's voice in a desperate tone cries out,

" MC come in please! MC, HQ, HQ! SOS! "

MC jolts out,

" Go Ahead, Rona, Loud and clear!"

Rona,

" Apollyon is missing! The time trod has malfunctioned and sent Apollyon to some unknown location here on the Planet. He had set the coordinate to a nearby city we were tracing to find a root causation then, just back a few days where a large population had gathered. After the time lever sparked out in a unfamiliar purple light beam he vanished into thin air. The city is all in flames and seems to be sinking into the sand. People are running everywhere in all directions away from the city in these rolling machines so we was attempting to find the cause of this devastation. We are presently in the middle east near a city called Dubai."

MC slings back,

" Rona calm down focus on the settings right before the accident occurred, also what is your coordinate right now and the date?"

Rona quickly transmits the coordinate/date to MC, as MC activates the local FTLs of that region to find Apollyon and quickly locates him all dressed on a tiny speck of a island Faror, about to sink. Rona reboots the Time trod just in time to transfer Apollyon off the tiny island back to her location and time right before He was about to mutate and swim back to land.

MC suggests to Rona,

" Rona set the time trod to launch back into orbit around the planet. Set a position half way between the Earth and the Moon. From here you will be out of the way of their satellites and the cloak will shield you from any detection at that range. Then create holoforms to transfer to the planet as will be much safer for now. "

" We have been having malfunctions here as well. As you already know by the last pinalog, Lucifer and Dawn has gone to Mars. At this point who knows what those two might be up to so keep your eyes peeled. Thy One will be here on the Mother Ship soon and maybe then we can straighten this mess out, OVER! "

Rona transmits,

" Roger that dodger it will be my pleasure to get back off this planet, ASAP, this darn thing is falling apart. The gravitational flux is bouncing like mad and these Earthoids have pulled so much Crude OIL out from under their crust the land is sinking into the cavities, OUT!"

Rona and Apollyon load into the time trod and set countdown sequence and in a flash beams off the planet up thru a dark evening cloud of dust and steam. The time trod inserts into orbit around the planet at the halfway mark as Rona launches one hundred more FTLs into the past eighteen months mainly inside all the major cities across the globe.

The images keep flooding in on all FTLs channels as the devastation mounts up as the FTLs trace back thru the past year of Earthoid 2012/2011C. E. Then suddenly a clear picture emerges from the FTL reporting in on September 12th 2011 CE. Rona turns to Apollyon and states,

" We need to start beaming our holoforms during this time span open up listening channels for specific areas and Apollyon prepare your holoform as well. "

Rona launches 112, more FTLs into that time window to get a better grasp on what triggered the events they had just witnessed. Suddenly a Votexicon point is established with a coordinate point and time. Rona transmitted the signal into the few Senerobots on board for the blem projector to reveal, then -----

"Ooo MY! GOD "

Rona shouts

" Apollyon forget the holoform, you have to go down there yourself something is happening in the deep oceans. Holoforms don't work to well in deep waters. So make like a Abyssopelastic and leave."

Rona sets the time trod to transcend to the location and drops Apollyon as he is mutating into the Ocean depths with several aquabots for life support into the mega depths. Rona hovers for a few minutes till the FTLs adjust to the sonics then she transcends back to the 114428 orbital insertion point to monitor the progress. She taps into an intercept from a Earthoid satellite 932,000 miles from Earth towards the Sun's Lagrange, where the Solar and Heliospheric Observatory is located. A massive solar flare erupts from the Sun directly towards the Earth.

Meanwhile back on board the, Mother Ship , Michael emerges from his chamber aware of all the happenings and joins MC at the main Bor station observatory as both stare silently into the blem accumulators as the data from the Rona's time trod pours in, then Micheal breaks the silence with a question?

" Shouldn't we of heard from Gabriel by now?"

MC responds,

" Yes, Mary just telepathed that Gabriel has experienced some trouble with the time trod as she called it, " Strange Gravity" Luckily THY was in transcended as they crossed paths. Both are near a star in a galaxy cluster the humanoids call, " Sagittarius Dwarf, " not to far from out present position , THY and Gabriel has swapped time trods and after a centrifugal slingshot beyond FTL speeds as both trods super enforced inertia, till Gab and THY spun out subspace both on track and should be reporting in soon. "

Michael nods his head in a very positive reinforcing gesture then adds,

" Michael knows Cflow has the ability to create Angellican beings but have also discovered from the vibcores THY one's holobeing gave me from Lucifer's blon study, that He also can create beings with Dawn One almost in the same manner, thus suspects that the Mars base Cydonia 400 BC has become a nest for, " Ludawnifers " A name Michael has coined to differentiate any supposed offspring that will migrate from that region as Senerobots have projected will occur."

MC denotes,

" Very well what do you recommend we do about this? "

Michael answers,

" We create a army. A army of Angellicans, THY One has agreed with this notion already in status. It has already become obvious that this ship is way under staffed and as unstable as this Galaxy is proving to be, we sure could use the extra help as you faithful one MC has alluded to already in foresight demologs."

MC questions,

" Just how big of an Army are you proposing Michael, the first commander, Captain of Angellicans? "

Michael responds,

" Ten Thousand "

MC turns to face Cflow and asked,

" Cflow just how long would it take to create 10,000 Angelicans? "

Cflow responds in time,

" Could replicate 10,000 Angelicans at full production long before we enter the Earthoid's solar system simply by creating 100 breeders within the embryonic cortex, as THY ONE can enter the, Be Fruitful and Multiply command when he arrives with the fresh DNA samples. "

MC responds,

" Wow! Talk about redesigning this ship we are about to undergo a major over haul as the Earthoids would say. OK Cflow lets get a count on the protomatter units we still have in storage. Will begin the schematics immediately. Cflow begin project 10,000 Angelicans Intergalactic Intervenors Immediately. "

Cflow responds,

" On it Roger Dodger MC, Master of Ceremonies. "

Cflow's projected holobeing disappears back into ether space as a deafly quiet falls over the Bor. MC and Michael glide over to the portals to watch the approaching, Sagittarius Dwarf as the data reads out a significant amount of dark matter has been displaced or simply missing along the simulated path of Lucifer's time trod into the Milky WAY galaxy main entry insertion point. THY One is back tracking along the displaced photonic pathway and is caught now within the time trod gravitron grabblers which tug the trod on board the Mother Ship is a flash, as THY ONE himself enters the corridor. Jubilation rings out all over the ship as MC greets THY ONE,

" Welcome Aboard, THY Master ONE, your absence is no longer appreciated. We are so grateful you have returned to us all safe and sound. "

THY ONE replies on the run then vapors,

" Roger that Dodger MC, no time for formal greetings must go into the THY ONE Blon immediately for matters are extreme and are at hand. "

In a flash THY ONE escapes into blon, then after a few seconds pass the whole ship, transcends as if a time trod deep inside the galaxy passing light years in a single bound. Suddenly the ship halts within a very beautiful solar system near this most wonderfully radiant planet glowing in a sweet purplish light yet iridescent by nature.

THY One on commtron broadcasting throughout the whole ship,

" We will establish shop here until repairs are made and MIchael's Army is created in it's full splendor. Contact Rona and channel this radiant energy from this star in this system through her time trod using the timelet FTLS immediately creating a laser of it to neutralize that emanate solar flare she has detected amassing, heading for Planet Earth ! Shrink ! Shrink ! shrink! "

Rona receives the beacon FTL with the alignment codes, she swings her trod about for channeling mode then slips back in time a few minutes before the prominence occurred and begins channeling the purple laser ions onto the pre- eruption site which absorbed a lot of the magnetic energy with greatly lessened the flare that was to occur before intervention, as Apollyon reports in to Rona,

" Wow! Apollyon here, cant believe my eyes but a huge underwater volcanic fissure has opened up in a deep ocean trench here about a mile wide in places. As far as Apollyon can see is boiling, magma emerging from the depths of the Earth. This isn't good the water is starting to boil as huge bubbles of gas and steam are forming. "

Rona transmits back to Apollyon,

" How deep is the trench and How high are the near by cliffs? "

Apollyon responds,

" The Aquabots have determined Apollyon is at coordinates 11.19'N 142.15' E Mariana Trench 35,994 below sea level at 16,155 P.S.I . It seems as if the ancient bottomless pit is opening up here. If it wasn't for the Aquabots Apollyon would be crushed imploded as a single atom. The cliffs rise up sharply to around 10,000 feet below sea level so some are over 25,000 feet high "

Rona relays all the Apollyon transmissions through the FTLs back to THY One for recommendations as her Time Trod remotes over the location Apollyon is submerged, "

**THY ONE thru timelets responds as his holoforms appears inside the time trod
with Rona,**

" OK we must bring down the cliffs over the bottomless pit before the chasm opens so wide that it cant be contained. The trick is doing this without creating a major tsunami, causing even more havoc to the region. We must channel the anti thermal fluid through the timelets pulling the heat out of the water freezing large thick sub plate sheets of Ice just below the cliffs then by channeling timelet lasers onto the cliffs the land mass will simply slide out onto the ice sheets as Apollyon and the Aquabots continually lower the sheets over the fissure for as long as it takes."

Rona chimes in,

" Yes! This can work we have all we need right here before us water for ice sheets, land mass, and anti thermal fluid, and the timelet particle laser, Kewel!"

Rona transcends the time trod below the ocean to the correct depth and begins the operation. The ocean begins to freeze into huge plates of ice sheets like underwater glaciers as the sub atomic laser begins eroding the cliff face sediments out onto them in layers like a mud slide. As one ice plate begins to lower another begins to form in slow secession slowly submerging into the boiling fissure deep below. The Mariana Trench begins to fill in and the bottomless pit is encapsulated as the, Cataclysm for now is averted.

Chapter five

Immaculate Conception

Meanwhile back on board the Mother Ship the jubilation is cut short as, Gabriel reports in from EYTAN WELL, Judea mountains, 30 BC,

" MC, MC ! Come in? Gabriel One here safely at Eytan Well camp down. "

MC responds,

" Great! Gabriel that is good news, very good news indeed! We have aligned the mission FTLs to your actually location so expect the time portal blem to open soon. This will allow you to monitor events along the continuum up to a 100 year window over several thousand miles up to around the year 70 AD. "

Gabriel responds,

" Very good, tuning mission timelets now. The signal seems to be very strong. Will send a DNA sample through soon to test the viability of the transporter, and yes, just thought would mention that this was one very sweet ride. "

" Roger that! "

MC relays,

“ The success of your mission is paramount, so THY One has pulled out all stops on this one. Also Gabriel be sure to set up the simulator to meld with the Senerobots. Once the correct blood line is located, begin the scan for the right family within the tribe for the encounter. “

Gabriel busy at the Command Bor within the timetrod for a few minutes setting up the mission systems then replies,

“ The timelets are verifying that the FTL subworm is established, so Gabriel will transcend outside the trod to collect some sample DNA for the test. “

MC,

“ Roger that Gab, be sure the trod is set to full evade mold, as well do not go wandering beyond the cloaking radius for we wouldn't want to alarm any animals or Earthoids by your sudden appearance into the earthordic continuum dimension. Cflow has finished producing the Vitrobot. Once the special DNA samples THY One brought back with him was introduced, so the package is ready awaiting your command when the time comes. “

Gabriel transcends just outside the trod and collects some DNA samples of several plants and insects and places them in a vile then re enters the trod. Inserts the samples into the timelet sub wave carriers. Almost immediately the samples appear on board the mothership ship transcending lightyears, now inside the lab receivers.

Cflow responds,

" Samples received in prefect condition. The test is complete all other mission systems here are ready and in standby mode awaiting Gabriel One's command for expedition. "

Gabriel back inside the time trod notices the Senerobots have identified the tribe with the richest blood line, and a FTL was already activated to surveill the group as one of the time beacons begins to blink.

Gabriel reports,

> **" Cflow seems we maybe to late for the couple that has been identified is older than the given age for Earthoid reproduction. "**

Cflow responds,

" We will modify the Vitrobot. Contact the couple using your holobeing as a dreamscape for they must be in on the plan. "

Gabriel responds,

" Roger that am on it, Am seeing a daughter of Aaron, and her name is Elizabeth. "

THY One at the main Bor intervenes,

" Gabriel we already know you will be successful for a advanced timelet FTL has just broadcast a message from the year 136 AD from the Earthoidic prospective which reads, "

THY One activates the Crynode which begins to read out loud,

“ In the days of Herod, king of Judea, there was a priest named Zechariah, of the division of Abijah. And he had a wife from the daughters of Aaron, and her name was Elizabeth. And they were both righteous before Elohim, walking blamelessly in all the commandments and statutes of the Lord. But they had no child, because Elizabeth was barren, and both were advanced in years. Now while he was serving as priest before Elohim when his division was on duty, according to the custom of the priesthood, he was chosen by lot to enter the temple of the Lord and burn incense. And the whole multitude of the people were praying outside at the hour of incense. And there appeared to him an angel of the Lord standing on the right side of the altar of incense. And Zechariah was troubled when he saw him, and fear fell upon him. “

“ But the angel said to him, "Do not be afraid, Zechariah, for your prayer has been heard, and your wife Elizabeth will bear you a son, and you shall call his name John. And you will have joy and gladness, and many will rejoice at his birth, for he will be great before the Lord. And he must not drink wine or strong drink, and he will be filled with the Holy Spirit, even from his mother's womb. And he will turn many of the children of Israel to the Lord their EL, and he will go before him in the spirit and power of Elijah to turn the hearts of the fathers to the children, and the disobedient to the wisdom of the just, to make ready for the Lord a people prepared." And Zechariah said to the angel, "How shall I know this? For I am an old man, and my wife is advanced in years." And the angel answered him, "I am Gabriel I stand in the presence of THY EL, and I was sent to speak to you and to bring you this good news. And behold, you will be silent and unable to speak until the day that these things take place, because you did not believe my words, which will be fulfilled in their time."

“ And the people were waiting for Zechariah, and they were wondering at his delay in the temple. And when he came out, he was unable to speak to them, and they realized that he had seen a vision in the temple. And he kept making signs to them and remained mute. And when his time of service was ended, he went to his home. After these days his wife Elizabeth conceived, and for five months she kept herself hidden, saying, " Thus the Lord has done for me in the days when he looked on me, to take away my reproach among people."

The Crynode fell silent as Gabriel falls back into his comforter in total amazement,

Thy one breaks the silence and pulls Gabriel from his dream by stating aloud,

“ Gabriel awake from your daydream! There is a problem we must not fail! The FTL has identified a disturbance in the continuum Elizabeth's John will be murdered before the mission can be completed so we must find a second earth bound Angelican to carry on the mission beyond John. “

“ THY One has detected a very unusual force at work here, and must consult with the, “ Ancient Ones at once. MC take over here the wheel ! “

MC replaces THY One at the main Bor station as THY escapes into personal blon in a flash.

Gabriel carries out his mission flawlessly. The prelude THY One presented was most helpful, yet a lull hung over the whole group awaiting the emergence of THY One from the blon with the advanced procedure that hopefully will circumvent the diverted causation module back into alignment with the main plan.

MC still at the main bor monitoring the advanced FTL through the timelets noticed a new signal coming in that verified THY One's concerns, thus activates the Crynode assigned to the moment,

" For King Herod had laid hold on John, and bound him, and put him in prison for Herodias' sake, his brother Philip's wife. For John said unto him, It is not lawful for thee to have her. And when he would have put him to death, he feared the multitude, because they counted him as a prophet. But when Herod's birthday was kept, the daughter of Herodias danced before them, and pleased Herod. Whereupon he promised with an oath to give her whatsoever she would ask. And she, being before instructed of her mother, said, Give me here John Baptist's head in a charger. And the king was sorry: nevertheless for the oath's sake, and them which sat with him at meat, he commanded it to be given her. And he sent, and beheaded John in the prison. And his head was brought in a charger, and given to the damsel: and she brought it to her mother. "

THY one reappears in the Bor besides MC with a proclamation,

" Gabriel we must intervene yet again for Lucifer will not be expecting a seconded Angellican. Trust me Lucifer has leaped into your timeline except slightly ahead of your continuum. "

" We will endow the next Angelican with some special powers that will supersede Lucifer in wit and wisdom. We must find another worthy young maiden along the blood line immediately Cflow is sending the new Vitrobot ! "

Gabriel scrambles the Senerobots back into the tribe's FTLs which traced the blood line for hours scanning many families way into the night from town to town, village to village, and even across the rural country side. Finally a beacon goes off near the town of Galilee.

Gabriel immediately quiets the beacon and pulls the FTL off line, deciding that He must go do this job alone with little detectable technology. Gabriel programs the textile replicators to materialize some clothing fitting for the times, gets dressed in the attire, grabs the new Vitrobot, transcends to a spot outside of Galilee near the suburb of Nazareth.

Gabriel emerges from the shadows and mingles into a crowd of people walking down the streets towards the house of Heli. The crowd moves on beyond Heli's House, as Gabriel exits the streets into the shadows again unnoticed along a hedged row. Until he came to a window where a lovely young lady was looking out at the stars. Gabriel said unto her that evening from the lawn,

" Hail, thou that art highly favoured, THY Lord is with thee: blessed art thou among women."

And when she saw him, she was troubled at his saying, and cast in her mind what manner of salutation this should be. And Gabriel said unto her,

" Fear not, Mary: for thou hast found favour with Elohim the Ancient Ones. And, behold, thou shalt conceive in thy womb, and bring forth a son, and shalt call his name, " Immanuel " He shall be great, and shall be called the Son of the Highest: and the Lord Thy EL shall give unto him the throne of his father David: And he shall reign over the house of Jacob for ever; and of his kingdom there shall be no end. "

Then said Mary unto Gabriel,

" How shall this be, seeing I know not a man?"

And the Angelican answered and said unto her,

" The Sacred Spirit shall come upon thee, and the power of the Highest shall overshadow thee: therefore also that sacred thing which shall be born of thee shall be called the Son of EL. And, behold, thy cousin Elisabeth, she hath also conceived a son in her old age: and this is the sixth month with her, who was called barren. For with Elohim nothing shall be impossible."

Gabriel releases the Vitrobot onto the window seal next to Mary with a gesture and a graceful smile. And Mary said,

" Behold the handmaid of the Lord; be it unto me according to thy word."

And Gabriel departed from her, once in the shadows and sensing no Earthoids transcends back aboard the timetrod. Gabriel shuts down all systems and falls off into a deep sleep so silent, so quiet not a single sound. Meanwhile back on the Mother Ship, Mary of the Heavens emerges from her personal blon and makes a statement,

" WOW! That went immaculately, I cant believe Lucifer is messing with our plans when he was the one that first suggested we carry out such a mission ? "

MC answers,

" Lucifer has his own agenda as has already been manipulating Earthoid events for eons by now. In fact our reconnaissance FTLs assigned to his movements have indicated a evolution in his abilities, Yet, Yet, Thy One persists that Lucifer still plays in some kind of grand scheme, so THY One has given him a new name, "Satariel" Whereas some can almost rival the abilities of THY One imagine that ! By the way Lady Mary One, fate has it that your counterpart was discovered in the process as you predicted. Your job is just beginning now that ours has commenced, as the Earthoids would say, " Underway! "

Mary One replies,

" Yes it is most peculiar that the pingalog acquisition assigned to Satariel is showing so much evidence that the Earthordic continuum is spewing off into several alternative time lines even as far back as the initial Adam and Eve insertion point. MC ! We need to activate a new project soon to counteract these repercussions. "

MC enthused,

" Yepper! Mary One, Cflow is already working on such a project. In fact we much withdraw Gabriel back into space to a point to where he can transcend to another insertion point pastronic to gain the advantage as a quantum diversion tactic sub loop tracking Satariel, now that we have identified a pattern mechanism. "

Mary shuttles,

" Very well! As always MC, Cflow, The Honorable Thy One, Micheal and Others with nameless faces developing within the embryological incubators."

" This mission is so important to this world that mere words cannot describe the vernaculars involved."

Cflow speaks,

“ Yes indeed Mary these missions are of the up most importance for if we are to actually save this world from total extinction, for we not only have a renegade Angelican on the loose but the futronics are indicating a shift in the gravitational paradigm that could destroy this planet in spite of all of our best efforts.”

Mary replies,

“ That sounds gruesome. No wonder Thy One has put some much energy into these projects. So if the worst case scenario develops ? What are our options ? “

MC divulges,

" For all those here, thoughts are that, we have come to this galaxy by accident according to our technological records, but THY One has assured that some other force is at work here. “

“ A ancient more primitive force that has brought us to this world for a reason, a purpose that we may not fully understand at this time. Yet we sense we all must do every thing in our power to help these Earthoids. THY One has just relayed a plan. One that may involve collecting Humanoids away from the planet if a global killer event becomes imminent, wherefores we must intervene and transcend actual people away from the planet predating such a nuclear holocaust, or natural upheaval. Cflow is working out the details as we speak. "

Cflow further responds,

" We are already preparing a place within range of the Earth if a mass exodus is to occur by the project name, Haven 2, actually a small moon in a solar system nearby the planet, yet has adequate elements to sustain the human beings from planet Earth. "

" The time trods are programmed, and soon some of the new Angelicans already evolving to maturity will man them transcending to Haven 2 for to establish biospheres. Once the spheres are founded the rapture will begin. Starting all across the time line certain Earthoids that meet the specifications will be transcended there. "

MC furthers,

" Indeed, Cflow this undertaking has great promise, but the prospects of averting a civilizational breakdown, but rather a major shift within the consciousness of Earthoids towards a sustainable peace time agri-planetary balance is still the main objective and from our advantage point if we stay vigilant this can be accomplished. We need more Angelicans down there on the surface. As the humans would say, More boots on the ground. "

Cflow responds,

" All in good time. We have made such good time, almost lost track of time. "

Mary sternly replies,

" So how much control do we have over Earthoid history, with advanced futronics? "

MC replies sternly,

" That My Dear, Remains to be seen! "

Mary stunned

" Remarkable!"

This is the end of the Volume One of The series ,

Alien Testament

Author- Timothy R. McBride

In the Year of Our LORD, 2010

Are we alone in the Universe?

The answer, " KNOW? "

www.ingramcontent.com/pod-product-compliance
Ingram Content Group UK Ltd.
Pitfield, Milton Keynes, MK11 3LW, UK
UKHW051137260726
13967UKWH00010B/3098

9 781458 312310